The Storybook

Adapted by Amy Jo Cooper

Based on the screenplay by
M. Night Shyamalan and Greg Brooker

23/8/0(

PUFFIN BOOKS

Published by the Penguin Group
Penguin Books Ltd, 27 Wrights Lane, London W8 5TZ, England
Penguin Putnam Inc., 375 Hudson Street, New York, New York 10014, USA
Penguin Books Australia Ltd, Ringwood, Victoria, Australia
Penguin Books Canada Ltd, 10 Alcorn Avenue, Toronto, Ontario, Canada M4V 3B2
Penguin Books (NZ) Ltd, Private Bag 102902, NSMC, Auckland, New Zealand

On the World Wide Web at: www.penguin.com

Penguin Books Ltd, Registered Offices: Harmondsworth, Middlesex, England

Published in Puffin Books 2000
7

On the World Wide Web at: www.stuartlittle.com

Set in AGaramond 15/21pt

Printed in the United Kingdom by Ebenezer Baylis

British Library Cataloguing in Publication Data
A CIP catalogue record for this book is available from the British Library
ISBN 0–141–30735–8

STUART LITTLE™

The Storybook

PUFFIN BOOKS

"It's today! It's today!" George Little cried, and leaped right in the middle of his parents' bed.

Today was the day the Littles were going to the orphanage to adopt the newest member of their family, a brother for George.

Today was also a school day. But all George could think about was his new brother. For weeks, he'd imagined all the fun they would have. They would play catch. They would wrestle. George had even decided he would teach him how to spit.

"But how will you know if you're picking the right one?" George asked as he boarded his school bus.

"We'll just know," his parents assured him and smiled.

As the bus pulled away, George leaned his head out the window and shouted, "Remember, I want a *little* brother. Not a big brother!"

Picking a child was more difficult than Mr and Mrs Little had expected. The orphanage was full of boys and girls. Mr and Mrs Little sat down on a bench and sighed.

"Oh, look at them," Mrs Little said.

"I know," Mr Little agreed. "They all seem so . . ."

". . . wonderful," Mrs Little completed his thought. (They did that a lot.)

"I think it's wonderful how you both know what the other one is going to say," a small, pleasant, voice piped up from below.

The Littles looked down. There, in front of them, stood a little orphan named Stuart, a really little orphan, no bigger than a mouse. In fact, he was a mouse, but a very well-mannered and thoughtful one.

Mr Little smiled and explained. "Yes, well, it happens when you've been together as long as we have as a . . ."

". . . family," Mrs Little finished and smiled.

Stuart smiled too. At that moment, the Littles knew exactly which child they would take home. They didn't even have to talk about it.

Mrs Keeper, the orphanage director, had her doubts, but the Littles had made up their mind. Stuart was a perfect fit for the Little family.

The Littles took Stuart into a bright yellow taxi, which took them across the river and through the town and Central Park to the Little family home on Fifth Avenue.

"They say every Little in the world knows how to find this house, even if they've never been here before," Mr Little proudly explained. "Something inside of them draws every true Little to where they belong."

At last, Stuart had a home!

Snowbell, the Littles' spoilt cat, didn't even bother to greet them when they arrived – until he smelled a mouse in the house. In a flash, Snowbell dashed into the hallway and snapped Stuart up.

Mr and Mrs Little ordered Snowbell to let Stuart go. Snowbell could not believe his ears. This mouse was a member of the family? It was more than Snowbell could bear.

George didn't take the news very well either. At first, he thought
his parents were joking. He had wanted a little brother, but not this
little. This wasn't a brother. This was a mouse!

George refused to talk to Stuart during dinner. Stuart pretended that nothing was wrong. But deep inside, his feelings were hurt, for he had really hoped that George would be his friend.

That night, the Littles gathered around the piano for a family sing-along. When Mrs Little started to play, she discovered that one of the keys was stuck.

"Maybe I can help?" asked Stuart.

Mr Little lifted the heavy piano top, and Stuart climbed inside

and crawled along the long rows of strings. He could see the broken key.

"Try it now," Stuart cried. Mrs Little played the song again. When she reached the note with the broken key, Stuart hit the key from the inside. The note sounded out loud and clear, and Mrs Little ended the song with a flourish.

George looked at his family and sighed. Then he hurried down to his basement retreat.

When it was bedtime, Stuart climbed under his gigantic covers and lay down. Everything in Stuart's room was human-size and much too big for Stuart, but he didn't mind at all.

"Goodnight, Stuart," said Mrs Little and kissed him on his tiny cheek.

"Goodnight, Mom. Goodnight, Dad." Stuart sighed and leaned back on to the enormous pillow.

What a wonderful end to a wonderful day.

The next day, Stuart woke with the sun and stretched. He yawned, took his toothbrush and comb, and walked into the bathroom. George was already there, brushing his hair and teeth. Stuart did the same, mimicking his brother.

"George, I'm trying to get the laundry started," Mrs Little called from downstairs.

George pulled off his pyjama top and dropped it on the floor with one swift motion – completely unaware that it landed right on top of Stuart.

"Hey!" Stuart shouted. But his tiny voice was muffled by the cloth.

Not hearing Stuart's shouts, George picked up his pyjamas, with Stuart bundled inside, and tossed them down the laundry chute.

Before Stuart knew it, he was sliding head first, on his belly, down the long, dark chute. He and George's pyjama top landed on a big pile of clothes.

Mrs Little plopped the pile of clothes into the washing machine, and turned it on. Water roared in all around Stuart. Soap bubbles tickled his nose. Stuart was trapped! He pounded on the glass door with his little paws.

Mrs Little looked up. *Is someone knocking on the door?* she thought. She put down a half-folded shirt and went to the front door. When she returned to the laundry room, she saw her littlest son pressed up against the washing machine door.

"Hi, Stuart," she said and gazed at him fondly. Then she realized what had happened to her son.

"Stuart!" she shouted in alarm and flung open the washing machine door. Stuart rode out on a wave of water and suds.

"I'm . . . OK, Mom . . ." he managed to cough out, blowing soap bubbles – and then he fainted.

Dr Beechwood assured the Littles that Stuart would be fine. The doctor warned that there were bound to be difficulties for a mouse in a human-size home. But there was some good news: Stuart was very clean now.

The next day, the Littles went to a large department store. They had decided to have a party to officially welcome Stuart into the family, and Stuart needed some new clothes.

In the shop window, George spied an expensive model sailboat called the *Lillian B. Womrath*. George couldn't take his eyes off the beautiful boat. It would surely win the model boat race that was to be held in Central Park.

At that moment, Anton, the school bully, walked out of the store.

"How do you like my new boat, George?" he teased and left with his pack of bratty friends.

"We never did finish building *your* boat, did we?" Mr Little said to George. "We'll race your boat next year."

"I'm not so good at the racing part," George replied.

"So what? You'll practise. It doesn't matter if you win. You try like heck and you have fun."

George looked doubtfully at his father, and then they all went inside the shop to buy clothes for Stuart.

Mrs Little led her family to the toy department. They were greeted
by a sales assistant who was very helpful with their request.

"Something formal, I think," Mrs Little suggested.

The salesman ducked behind the counter and placed several

selections of Ben dolls on the counter: Barbados Ben, Chef Ben, Lumberjack Ben, Gladiator Ben and Polo Ben.

Stuart tried on every outfit and was quite pleased with his new wardrobe.

The whole Little clan showed up for the party.

"Little hi, Little lo!" Mr Little greeted.

"Little hey, Little ho!" they replied.

Stuart watched the family greeting ritual from the top of the stairs. *Boy, that's a lot of Littles*, he thought to himself. His stomach fluttered with nerves. He took a deep breath and started down the stairs.

"Attention, everyone," his mother called. "This is Stuart."

The entire Little family looked towards the stairs. Then they looked down.

Edgar Little was the first to speak. "Why he's a -"

"- dorable! Absolutely adorable!" Aunt Beatrice declared.

The relatives showered Stuart with gifts – a bicycle, a football, skis – all of which were far too big for Stuart. Stuart knew it was the thought that counted, and he was overwhelmed by their kindness. In the orphanage, he and the other children used to tell fairy tales to each other about finding their families. And about having a party just like this one.

"I don't know much about families," Stuart announced, "but this must be the nicest one in the world. I want to thank each of you, because now I know that fairy tales are real."

When the Littles took a group photo, the only ones not smiling were Snowbell and George. As far as they were concerned, Stuart had no business being a Little. Besides, how was Snowbell ever going to hide the fact that he had a mouse for a master?

That night, Mr and Mrs Little worried that they might have made a mistake adopting Stuart. Stuart had his doubts too. Although he was very happy, he wondered if he really fitted in.

Stuart crawled into his parents' bed, waking them up. He asked if they could find out about his family. The ones he looked like. Stuart felt something missing inside him. It was an empty space that needed to be filled.

The Littles agreed to help Stuart find out about his mouse parents, but his request dismayed and disappointed them. For they loved Stuart as their own, and it broke their hearts to think they might lose him.

They spoke to Mrs Keeper the very next day.

A few days later, Stuart found Snowbell in the pantry.

"Snowbell, I think we got off on the wrong paw. Want to be friends?" Stuart asked eagerly.

"Umm . . . no," Snowbell replied and strode into the kitchen. "Mice! Can't live with them – can't eat them."

Just then, Monty, a hungry alley cat, leaped through Snowbell's kitchen cat-flap. Monty and the other street cats regularly raided the Littles' pantry, whether Snowbell liked it or not. Their gang was led by Smokey, the meanest cat in the city.

"How about a little nibble?" Monty asked and pushed open the pantry door.

Snowbell sighed with relief. Stuart was nowhere in sight. If the alley cats knew about Stuart, he was one cooked kitty.

"Well, I hate to eat and run . . ." Monty trailed off, suddenly springing on to the counter where Stuart was busy with a box of snacks.

Stuart politely introduced himself to the menacing cat.

"I'm not just a mouse," he explained. "I'm a member of this family."

"A mouse with a pet cat?" Monty laughed.

The humiliation was more than Snowbell could bear. With claws out and teeth bared, he lunged at Stuart and chased him all around the kitchen.

Snowbell cornered Stuart against the basement door. The cat smiled. At last he had him! But Stuart sucked in his breath and squeezed himself under the door. He tumbled down the cellar stairs to safety.

Stuart stared in amazement at George's basement hideaway. In every corner and on every surface were models, all built by George and his father. There were small models of classic cars lined up on a shelf. On a table was a model city street with shops and tiny people.

There were horses and wagons, a train, and even a hydroelectric dam. They were beautiful. And best of all, they were all Stuart's size.

Stuart convinced George to let him play with the models. Soon, they were having so much fun that George even forgot Stuart was a mouse. Stuart was happy too. It was the first time that he'd fitted in since he'd arrived.

Mr and Mrs Little were more than surprised when they checked on their sons. The two boys were busy working on George's sailboat, the *Wasp*. With Stuart's help, George was going to finish it. And together they were going to race her!

That night, Monty introduced Snowbell to Smokey, the alley cat leader.

"Monty says you can help," Snowbell stammered.

"A mouse with a pet cat!" Smokey shouted. "A cat cannot have a rodent for a master."

Snowbell explained that if something happened to Stuart, the Littles would blame him. He would be kicked out. If they got rid of Snowbell, they would get rid of the cat-flap. No cat-flap, no more snacks for the alley cats.

"Don't worry, Tinkerbell. I'll fix it," Smokey concluded.

It was the day of the race. George and Stuart stood by the side of the large pond in the middle of Central Park.

"I'm glad you're here, George, someone's got to finish last," Anton taunted. In his arms was the *Lillian B. Womrath*.

George had no time to think about Anton. He handed Stuart the remote control while he lowered the *Wasp* into the water.

The remote was almost as big as Stuart. He reeled under its weight into the crowd. Someone knocked into Stuart, and the remote control went flying. It was crushed by a passerby before Stuart could reach it.

George was heartbroken. Stuart started to apologize, but George just walked away. Mr and Mrs Little hurried after him.

"All boats to their marks! Ready! And go!" shouted the starter.

The crowd squealed in delight as the boats set sail. The starter's voice rose over the cheers of the crowd, "Sails are full – and there's a mouse on that boat!"

George and his parents stopped in their tracks. They pushed their way back through the crowd. Stuart was sailing the *Wasp* – in the wrong direction!

Stuart finally gained control of the sails and turned the *Wasp* around. The boat soon picked up speed. Just past the bridge, the *Womrath* crashed into some of the other boats and pushed its way ahead of the pack. Stuart quickly pulled away from the jam and the *Wasp* was soon gaining on the leaders.

At the halfway buoy, the *Wasp* was neck and neck with the *Womrath*.

Anton wasn't happy. He didn't like to lose, especially to a mouse. He set the *Womrath* on a collision course with the *Wasp*.

"Stuart, look out!" George warned.

But it was too late. Anton's boat collided with the *Wasp*, causing a terrible tangle.

Stuart climbed the treacherous rigging and managed to free his mast.

"I hope that mouse can swim," Anton sneered and steered his boat into the *Wasp*'s path again.

Miraculously, Stuart managed to avoid the collision. He pointed the *Wasp* towards the finish line – while the *Womrath* crashed into the rocky edge of the pond.

Under the direction of her brave little captain, the *Wasp* easily won the race.

The crowd broke into a big cheer as Stuart hopped ashore.
"Who is that mouse?" someone asked.
"That's no mouse," George proudly replied. "That's my brother!"

There were great festivities that night at the Littles' house. All of the relatives celebrated Stuart's triumph. It was the happiest moment of his life.

The doorbell rang, and Mr Little went to answer it. Standing in the doorway was a middle-aged mouse couple: Reginald and Camille Stout. They said they were Stuart's mouse parents.

Mr and Mrs Little had a serious talk with the Stouts. The Stouts said that they couldn't afford to feed Stuart when he was born. They had had to give him up for adoption. But now they wanted him back.

The Littles had no choice but to let the Stouts take Stuart. They loved Stuart dearly, but they wanted to do what was best for him – even if that meant breaking their own hearts in the process.

George thought the idea stank. Stuart belonged with the Littles. George stormed out of the room and locked himself in the basement.

Stuart's dream was over. The fairy tale had come to an end. Sadly, he packed up his belongings and left with the Stouts.

With tears in his eyes, George joined his parents outside and gave Stuart his model sports car. Then he ran back to the house and cried himself to sleep on Stuart's bed.

The three mice piled into the little car and drove away. Stuart pressed his face against the back window and waved goodbye. When Mr and Mrs Little waved back, his heart filled with sorrow. He watched as the Littles' house disappeared from view.

"Is this paradise or what?" Mr Stout asked Stuart when they arrived at his new home.

Stuart looked around. They were on the ninth hole of a miniature golf course. The course was right in the middle of an abandoned amusement park. It wasn't exactly paradise. A lump formed in Stuart's throat as he surveyed his surroundings.

Later that night, Stuart looked out the window from his room. Scraps of paper scuttled across the deserted paths. The empty park seemed so desolate and lonely. In the distance, the lights of New York City twinkled. To Stuart, it was the most beautiful sight in the world. In the midst of that mass of buildings was the one place Stuart called home.

Three days after the Stouts took Stuart away, Mrs Keeper visited the Littles. She had news about Stuart's parents. They had been in an accident in a greengrocers.

"They didn't make it," Mrs Keeper solemnly informed them.

When the Littles found out that the accident had happened years ago, they were horrified. The Stouts were not Stuart's parents after all. He had been mousenapped! Mr and Mrs Little decided to take the matter up with the police.

Detective Sherman and Detective Allen took down all of the information on Stuart. The situation didn't look very promising. The Littles worried that they would never see Stuart again.

That was exactly what Snowbell, Monty and Smokey wanted. Now that the Stouts' story had been revealed, there was only one thing left to do. They had to scratch Stuart out. Smokey put every cat in the city on alert.

That night, Mr and Mrs Stout took a drive through the deserted park. Stuart sat quietly in the back seat. He could hear his mother crying.

Stuart tried to reassure her. "Mom, now that I'm a Stout again, I'll always be here to take care of you, because that's what families do."

Mrs Stout couldn't take it any more. "Tell him the truth!" she shrieked to Reginald, who told Stuart how Smokey and his gang had threatened them unless they pretended to be his parents. Tonight they were on their way to hand Stuart over. But they just couldn't go through with it – not after hearing Stuart's kind words.

"You lied and cheated? That's wonderful!" Stuart shouted. "That's why I've been feeling so sad. I'm not a Stout. I'm a Little. I'm Stuart Little!"

Without waiting one moment longer, Stuart got behind the wheel of the sports car.

"Goodbye, Fake Father! Goodbye, Fake Mother!" he shouted, and headed home.

Meanwhile, the Littles had been searching everywhere for Stuart. They stopped by the police station, but the detectives still had no news. They were fairly certain that the Littles would never see their son alive again.

Sadly, Mr and Mrs Little returned from the police station. George came running out of the basement. In his hands, he had a pile of papers. They were posters he had made describing Stuart.

"Look, it has our phone number and our address and there's even a reward," he said excitedly and held a poster up for his parents to see.

George wanted to put the posters up all over the city. All of the Little relatives had come out to help. There was only one problem. The posters didn't have Stuart's picture on them.

"The family portrait," Mrs Little suggested, and George eagerly got out a pair of scissors and cut Stuart out of the picture.

Once the job was done, all the Littles bundled up and headed out into the night to put up George's posters. They hoped they would help bring Stuart home.

After Stuart left the Stouts, he steered his little sports car back to Central Park. Stuart didn't know exactly which way to go, but deep down he knew that he could find his way home.

Every Little in the world can find the Little house, he thought over and over again.

Through the silence of the empty park, Stuart heard an ominous noise: *click, click, click*. Smokey and three street cats had surrounded Stuart's car!

Stuart revved the engine and sped backward away from the cats. The car flew off the path, rolled down a hill and into a drainpipe, finally landing in a huge pool of water.

Stuart gasped for air and tried to stay afloat. He grabbed his suitcase and climbed aboard, waving goodbye to the cats behind him. The water swirled faster as Stuart approached a deadly drop. He jumped to safety just before his suitcase hurtled down the waterfall.

Exhausted and wet, Stuart pulled himself out of the drain and looked down the street. Before him was the most wondrous sight – the Little house. It was true. Every Little can find his way home!

Stuart scampered up the stairs and crawled through the letter box. The only one home was Snowbell, who convinced Stuart that the Littles didn't love him any more.

"Ever since you left, it's just movies, parties, roller skating,

amusement parks. They're having the time of their lives," Snowbell explained.

At first, Stuart didn't believe him, but Snowbell showed him the family portrait and the hole where Stuart's picture used to be.

"I should've known. It was too good to be true," Stuart sighed and sadly left the Little house for good.

Stuart was miserable. He shuffled back through the park to the boat pond.

After Stuart left, Snowbell started to think about how miserable the Littles really were. He had to find Stuart. Stuart was family after all, and the Littles loved him as much as they loved Snowbell. His cold heart melted just in time.

Snowbell found Stuart sitting high up in a tree in the park. He climbed up beside Stuart and tried to persuade him to return home. The alley cats were just a few steps behind him.

Sad and tired of running, Stuart called to them from his perch. "Hey, guys! Come on up here so we can get this over with!"

The cats didn't wait for a second invitation. They pounced on the tree trunk and went after Stuart.

"Stuart, what are you doing?" Snowbell cried, as he carried Stuart higher up into the tree to safety. "I lied before. George misses you. You have to go home."

"Let's call this whole thing off. Stuart is family," he explained to the cats.

"Boys, scratch 'em both," Smokey ordered.

Thinking quickly, Stuart removed Snowbell's collar and looped it on a nearby branch.

"Try and catch me!" he dared and slid to the end of the branch where he dangled helplessly.

Luckily, the cats' tree branch broke, sending them tumbling into the pond below.

"Hang on, Stuart. I'll get you," Snowbell called and turned around – only to find himself face to face with Smokey.

Smokey hissed and arched his back. He was just about to swipe a deadly claw at Snowbell, when Stuart pulled himself up and swatted Smokey with a tree branch. Knocked off balance, Smokey plummeted down and joined his gang in the cold pond.

Snowbell and Stuart had saved each other!

Back at home, the Littles were overjoyed to see Stuart. And from that moment on, Mr and Mrs Little, George, Stuart and Snowbell were one *little*, happy family.